This Little Tiger book belongs to:

_____

_____

_____

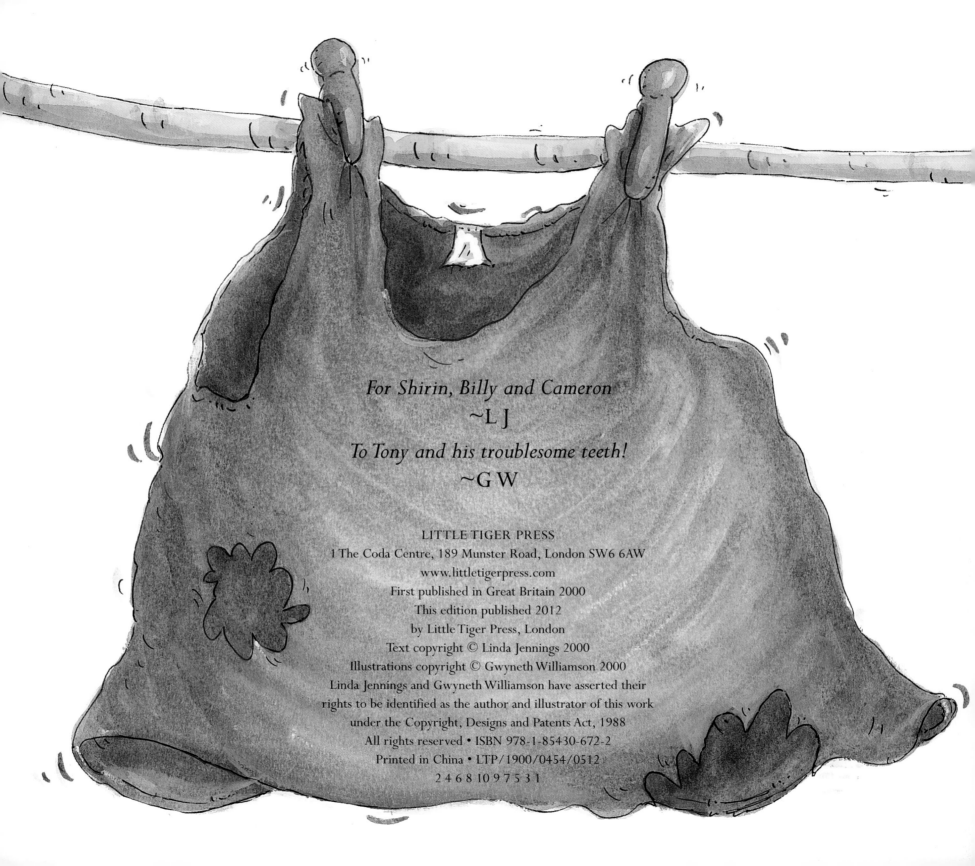

For Shirin, Billy and Cameron
~ L J

To Tony and his troublesome teeth!
~ G W

LITTLE TIGER PRESS
1 The Coda Centre, 189 Munster Road, London SW6 6AW
www.littletigerpress.com
First published in Great Britain 2000
This edition published 2012
by Little Tiger Press, London
Text copyright © Linda Jennings 2000
Illustrations copyright © Gwyneth Williamson 2000
Linda Jennings and Gwyneth Williamson have asserted their
rights to be identified as the author and illustrator of this work
under the Copyright, Designs and Patents Act, 1988
All rights reserved • ISBN 978-1-85430-672-2
Printed in China • LTP/1900/0454/0512
2 4 6 8 10 9 7 5 3 1

Titus's Troublesome Tooth

Linda Jennings and Gwyneth Williamson

LITTLE TIGER PRESS

Titus the Goat ate everything.
He ate carrots and cabbages.

He ate dandelions
and daisies.

He ate prickly,
tickly thistles . . .

. . . and he even ate Farmer
Harry's pants and vests
off the washing line!

Titus absolutely loved
eating, until one day . . .

. . . he woke up with a terrible pain.

He didn't want his breakfast . . .

and he didn't want to munch and crunch the apples in the orchard.

He wasn't even tempted to
nibble at Mrs. Harry's nightgown.
Titus felt as miserable as . . .

. . . well, as miserable as a goat with toothache!
He was a very grouchy, grumbly goat indeed.

"That's a troublesome tooth," said Danny the Donkey.
"Open your mouth and I'll pull it out with my big, strong teeth."

Titus shook from his
horns to the tip of his tail.
"Ooh-er, no thanks," he bleated.
He ran and ran and grouched
and grumbled . . .

. . . until he reached the farmyard.

"That's a troublesome tooth," said Sadie
the Hen. "Open your mouth and I'll peck
it out with my nice, sharp beak."

Titus quivered on all four hooves.
"Ooh-er, no thanks," he cried.

Titus ran and ran and grouched
and grumbled . . .

. . . until he reached the barn. "That's a troublesome tooth," said Polly the Cat. "Open your mouth and I'll scratch it out with my long, shiny claws."

Titus trembled from his white beard to his furry bottom. "Ooh-er, no thanks," he shouted.

Titus ran and ran and grouched and grumbled . . .

. . . until he reached
the meadow.
"That's a troublesome
tooth," said Basil the Bull.
"Open your mouth and I'll butt it out
with my hard, curly horns."

Titus's teeth chattered and rattled.
"Ooh-er, no thanks," he sobbed.
Titus ran and ran and grouched
and grumbled . . .

. . . until he reached the duck pond.

"That's a troublesome tooth," said Daphne the Duck.

"Open your mouth and I'll tug it out with some duckweed."

Titus shook so much that he nearly fell into the water.

"Ooh-er, no thanks," he yelled.

Titus ran and ran and grouched and grumbled . . .

. . . until he found himself right back in the farmyard again.

"Don't worry," said Sadie the Hen.

"Farmer Harry will get rid of
that troublesome tooth for you,
because he's called the Vet!"

"The Vet!"
shouted Titus.

He quivered and he shivered, he trembled and he shook. His teeth rattled and chattered.

"No way do I want *the Vet!*"

Titus ran and ran

and grouched

and grumbled until . . .

and the troublesome
tooth fell out at last!